Nicola Hun
christmas '06

THE GREEN MAN

THE GREEN MAN

An Eternity

by

JANE GARDAM

Illustrated by

MARY FEDDEN

THE WINDRUSH PRESS • GLOUCESTERSHIRE

First published in Great Britain in 1998
by The Windrush Press
Little Window, High Street,
Moreton-in-Marsh,
Gloucestershire GL56 0LL

Telephone: 01608 652012
Fax: 01608 652125
Email: WindrushPress@Netcomuk.co.uk

ISBN 1 900624 21 4

Printed and Bound in Slovenia
by Printing House Delo-Tiskarna
by arrangement with Korotan, Ljubljana

The Green Man *is* no enemy of Christ

fedden 1998

1

THE GREEN MAN

THE Green Man stood in the fields. In the darkness of winter he was only a shadow.

People going to the tip to throw away their Christmas trees noticed the shadow as their cars sped down the lanes. 'That shadow,' they said. 'Over there.'

Later, in January, the shadow looked like a stump or a post. 'Tree struck by lightning over there,' they said as they rushed along to work at the power-station across the fields. 'Unsightly looking thing.' If they were local people who had lived there some time, they said, 'Look, there's that stump thing again. Strange how you never seem to notice until it's back.'

When blowy March came and the days seemed to lighten over the dunes, you could hear the sea tossing and see it spouting up, people on their way to early holidays across the water and beyond the Alps would say, 'Well, someone's been planting seeds. There's a scarecrow. Spring will likely come.'

For the Green Man would now be standing with arms astretch and head askew and all his tatters flying, blustering grey and black and dun against the dun fields and the grey sky and the black thorn-bushes. There was beginning to be something rakish and reckless now about the Green Man.

Then in April the Green Man stood forth in cold sunshine, his hands folded over the top of his hoe and his chin on his hands, and in the dawn light of Eastertime people talking or jogging or riding by, eating things and laughing, quarrelling, shouting and singing, saw him there clearly, and bright green.

His old black clothes looked green and his winter skin looked bronze-green like a Malay's. His eyes were amber-green and one minute you saw him, and the next minute you didn't.

'Did you see that man!?'

'What man?'

'That man over there in that field. No - too late. It's gone now. Like a statue. Gold. No, green.'

'It must be advertising something.'

'Did you see that man?' the children cried, looking backwards from car windows, and the grown-ups went on talking or didn't bother to answer.

The old country people would say, 'Maybe it's the Green Man.'

'What's the Green Man?'

'Nobody knows. He's some man that's always been around here. I used to see him when I was little. I'd have thought he'd be dead by now.'

'The Green Man?' the granny would say. Then: 'Never! It couldn't be. I used to see the Green Man when I was a child and, even then, there was talk of him being as old as time. He had other names, too. He lived hereabouts somewhere.'

Then a leery, queery old voice from somebody wrapped up in the back of the car among the babies - it would be something after the nature of a great-grandfather - would say, 'I seed the Green Man wunst when I were in me bassinette in petticoats. We called him Green Man, or mebbe Wildman. And my old Pa, he said his old Pa seed the Wild Green Man one day. It was the day my old greaty greaty grandpop went marching long this lane in his cherry-coloured coat, to the field of Waterloo.'

'The only Green Man I know,' the Dad would say as he drove the car, far too fast, round corners of the lane that, after all, were once only right-angled bends around the fields, 'is a pub,' and he'd rush them along towards the motorway that joined up with the Channel Tunnel or the ferry.

'If it was the Green Man,' the children would sometimes say as they stood on the deck of the ferry and looked back at the sparkling white cliffs with their grass-green icing, 'however old can he be? He could be a hundred.'

Nobody knew.

And nobody knows.

Under different names the Green Man may be a thousand years old. Or ten thousand. But his eyes are young and bright and by the time it's midsummer he is looking dangerously attractive and permanent. He has never had a grey hair in his green head. In his sea-green eyes of July is a far-away magical gaze if you can get near enough to see it. But it is hard to get near. Now you see him, now you don't. The field is empty and you'll be lucky to catch a glimmer of a face between branches, down the coppice. Did you see a figure at work with a bill-hook by the blackthorn in white bloom? Maybe you didn't.

Or he may pass you silently on the dyke above, when you're fishing the field-drains. In the warm dusk at the top of summer he is like the nightingale and gone for deep woodland places. At dawn he is like the skylark, a speck on the blue sky.

Do not imagine that the Green Man is soft and gentle on his land. For all his stillness he is given to rages. He likes to observe and see things right.

'Get off your backsides,' he has been known to roar, 'Keep to your element.' He shouts this at seed-time and harvest, yells at those - there aren't many - who know him well.

Sadie and Patsy and Billy, the next-farm children, know him well, and they hang around him and huggle his legs and ankles. They tickle the bare place between his boots and his trouser bottoms, they tease him with teazles.

'Get off your backsides and out of this drill,' yells the Green Man at these babies. 'This drill!' he yells.

A drill is a long straight furrow in the earth into which the seeds are trickled and then covered up. The Green Man makes thousands of drills across the earth until it looks like corduroy cloth. The seeds grow and turn into one thing or another. They whiten with tendrilly peas, they turn green-gold with barley. Barley whiskers are the colour of a princess's hair.

'Get off my land,' bellows the Green Man as he sees the cat coming, on tip-toe, paddling and playing, chewing at the barley stalks in the heat.
'Get off my back,' he thunders next, as the cat comes lapping and weaving and purring and winding around him, growling like a motor, springing up all-claws

Fedden 195

to land like needles on the Green Man's shoulders and even his head. Very bad language follows then. 'Get off, you filthy scat-scumfish cat. Each to his *element*.'

The cat drops off the Green Man and lies on its back and shows the Green Man its fluffy white stomach and grins up at him. All animals are interested in the Green Man, but he by no means treats them like pets.
And he doesn't treat people like pets.

As the year passes the Green Man keeps away from people more and more. In high summer deep in the trees, he watches, very stiff and silent.
He will watch in secret.

You can see carvings of him in churches like this. Watching you. It has always been so. He has always been there. Sometimes he is a leaf-mask on a frieze. Sometimes he looks like leaves only.

2

THE GREEN MAN MOUNTS A

MOUSE HUNT

THE Green Man keeps a house for comfort, but he's very seldom inside it. He has had wives in his time, maybe hundreds, and they have tried to care for it. One wife cannot have been long-since, for he has twelve sons and four daughters living, very sturdy. Of course they may be much older than they look.

The twelve sons are scattered about the world, as sons tend to be, but the four daughters visit regularly, as daughters are more likely to do. The house is like a lark's nest lying low in the fields. The doors and the windows of the house are always open until the daughters close them. They visit, bringing bread and milk and lamb-chops and shortbread, cleaning-fluids, dish-cloths and porridge. They flick about with feather dusters and say, 'This place gets no better. Lord how it smells of mice!' They go looking for their father in the flicker of the poplars and down the marsh and across the fields near the sea.

The mice are not in the house at all on these occasions. Mice can smell daughters as daughters can smell mice. When they hear the daughters' cars arriving, their noses twitch and they're off into the bushes.

But when the daughters have gone away again, the mice creep greedily back. The mice are fieldmice but this is a misnomer. They should be called pantrymice or cupboardmice or pocketmice. They run in the Green Man's chests of drawers and armoires; in his bags of meal and flour.

They run among the dish-cloths and in the Green Man's little-used blanket. They lie, fat and lazy, in the fold of his folded deck-chair. They nestle in his boots and nest in his woollen cardigan and in the pocket of the macintosh that hangs on the back of his kitchen door.

Do not imagine that the Green Man is a saint to these mice.

The weather one Spring was cruelly sharp and perhaps the Green Man was feeling the weight of his two or three thousand years. He was using his house for sleeping every night. He was even occasionally lighting his dangerous paraffin stove which lit with a pop and a blob.

One day he lay down on his couch in the day-time, sneezing, with his cushion and his rug. He felt heavy with years and he coughed as he slept. And awoke to the mice running across his face like rain. He felt them running about in his blanket and snuffling at his toes. There was activity in his green-gold hair. With a roar he lit the lamp and found a mouse making off with a green curl to her nest in his boot.

'This must end!' cried the Green Man. 'The time has come. Each to his *element*,' and the next day he set off down the lane with his cheque-book and confronted the corn-chandler's in the High Street of the nearest market town. The corn-chandler's stands between the supermarket and the popso-bar, but it does a good trade.

How very strange the Green Man looked, holding out his cheque-book, demanding a writing implement. 'Mouse-Poison,' cried the Green Man. 'A quantity.'

Someone ran into the yard and called in others. 'There's a right one here.'

'Who is it? What is it? Where's it from? Is it human? Why's it green?' The old pale-faced corn-chandler sat by the fire in the back of the office. 'It'll be the Green Man,' he said.

'Is it the Council? Is it political? Is it trouble?'

'It's the Green Man.'

'He's for killing mice, he's no *green* man. Is he out of a fairground?'

'Don't thwart him,' said the corn-chandler. 'Don't thwart the Green Man,' he said, poking the fire.

Fedden 1998

The Green Man walked home along the ice-rutted lanes and the cold air puffed from his mouth like a dragon. 'Mice,' he muttered. 'Mice. Each to his element,'

When he reached home he called, 'This is to fettle you. Back to your fields,' and he lifted the lid of the flour kist and saw fat, snoring, distended mice, from weeks back, lying like drunken skiers in the snow. They looked comfortable and in bliss.

These were the ones who were still sleeping and hadn't realised yet that the more flour they ate, the less likely they would be to get out. There were a number of dead ones. The Green Man tipped the whole brigade out into the grass. The ones who could still snore woke up and made off, looking foolish. The foolish look of the released mice amused the Green Man, and he liked them after all as they ran away. Then he looked with shame at the mouse poison in the great drum he had bought from the corn-chandler. Where to put it for safety until he could take it back and swap it for seed?

He put the drum inside the flour crock for the moment and went off to the fields where he stood planning the year in the March weather.

The Green Man can make mistakes, for he is a man.

3

THE GREEN MAN GOES TO THE SEASIDE

Usually the Green Man keeps away from the ocean. He likes the drains and dykes and goits and runnels that water his land and the green rushes that spike them. He watches the arrows of the water-voles, the mirror the water makes for sailing swans or flying geese. The eyes of these creatures watch the Green Man as he passes. None of them comments.

But beyond the dykes and the marsh is the sea, which is not the natural element of the Green Man. Sometimes when a sheep strays to the strand he has to go down there looking for it, but the sea feels hostile and full of anachronisms.

Most of all the Green Man detests mermaids. Whenever he is forced to go anywhere near the sea he keeps his eyes off the rocks.

'Yoo-hoo, coo-eee,' call the mermaids, giggling and twiddling their golden ringlets through their fingers, 'Who can't swim then, Lover-boy?' Two of the mermaids are called Ermyntrude and Cayley.

'Coooeee, Green Man, you don't dare touch us.'

'Half and halves,' mutters the Green Man. 'No sense of their element.' He watches his dog, and only his dog. His dog is flurrying the sheep home. 'Neither wet nor dry,' snarls the Green Man. 'Beyond my understanding.'

Fodden 1998

But one day the mermaids are so provocative and insolent that the Green Man turns and walks right into the sea.

Ermyntrude and Cayley are so surprised they forget to slither away, and sit with their pouty little mouths each in an oh! They throw up their hands, ooh la! Ermyntrude's golden comb decorated with limpets falls into the sea.

The Green Man seizes the two mermaids, one under each arm. Abandoning the sheep and his dog he marches back over the dry land, leaving marsh and dykes and drains behind him. Two gliding swans behold him from the water and raise their eyebrows. 'Help, help,' squeak the percussive mermaids, and wave their little white arms out front, their tails wagging, slap, slap behind.

The Green Man goes into his house and tucks both mermaids under one arm for a moment while he fills up the bath tub from the keg. Then he slings the pair of them in.

'Sit there,' he says, 'till I think what to do with you. Each to his element. Find what it is.'

He goes off to dig his potatoes.

'He's coming back again,' say the water-voles. They had caught sight of his retreating figure before, and thought he had been very successfully fishing.

He's coming back again,' says the next door farmer (Jackson) who is the grandson of Sadie long ago. He had seen the Green Man pass, but only from the front. 'He's abducting women now,' he says. 'This might be nasty.'

Jackson goes into the Green Man's house and sees two girls' heads looking over the edge of the bath tub. When they see the next-door farmer they begin to giggle and sing so that he says, 'Well! So you were willing were you? I'm disgusted,' and slams off.

The water-voles tell it all to some seagulls. Seagulls think they are nobody's fool. They take nothing on trust. They fly to the bathroom window and look in. Twirling fishtails whirlpool the water. 'Couple of fish,' they report. 'No worries.'

The four daughters of the Green Man happen to be visiting that day and they are surprised to see the mermaids in the bath tub. By this time the mermaids are growing tetchy and needing salt.

'There'll be big damages for this,' screeches Ermyntrude.

'It's a scandal,' squawks Cayley, 'It's a threat to the Environment. Haphazard! Erratic! He's a danger to the Community. *Green Man* my tail.'

Fedden 1998

The daughters found a small tin hip-bath, filled it with tank water and took the mermaids, one at a time, back to the sea. The tide had gone out and they had a long walk. Each mermaid delivered a separate scolding all the way, protesting that it was dangerous for them to be separated, and similar rubbish.

'Shut up,' said the daughters, 'or we'll drop you in the shallows and you'll have to wriggle off like eels in an ungainly way.'

'Stuff you all,' said the mermaids as they each glided quickly into the deep.

The daughters noticed the Green Man digging his potatoes as, carrying the empty hip-bath, they returned from the sea for the second time and they were so cross with him that they passed him by without speaking. When they were back in the house though, they made tea and caught each others' glance and couldn't stop laughing.

'You should have sliced them in half,' said the Green Man coming in, 'I was thinking of it. Mermaid-tail fillet is a little-known delicacy, too sensible a concept for fairy-tale.'

'It is a fairy tail,' said the most amusing of the daughters but all the others - and the Green Man - groaned.

'And you thought to be a conservationist!' said the eldest daughter.

'I don't know why,' said the Green Man, 'most of it's guesswork. Folk-lorists. Folk-laureates' (now the amusing daughter groaned). 'Each to his element,' said the Green Man. 'No messing.'

The mermaids were no bother to the Green Man after this. Ermyntrude's golden comb with the limpets was washed up at Ramsgate, and sold at a boot fair.

Fedden 1998

4

THE GREEN MAN GOES WITH THE DEVIL

TO THE MOON

It was one evening in summer when the Green Man met the Devil under an apple tree in the orchards.

'I'd heard you favoured fruit,' said the Green Man, offering him a Worcester Pearmain.

'Good evening,' said the Devil with a charming, quizzical look, 'I'd been hoping we'd meet.'

The Green Man looked hard at the Devil and thought, 'But this must be a looking-glass. He is just like me.'

The Green Man walked all round the apple tree and examined the Devil from every side. It could not be a looking-glass because the Green Man could see the back of the Devil's neck which was creased with lines as deep as the bark of an old tree. He felt the back of his own neck and found them there, too.

Coming round in front again he watched the Devil picking his pointed teeth with a twig, and saw that the Devil's eyes were his own eyes at certain times or phases of the moon. They were watchful and knowing and on the hypnotic side. Yellow-gold like a goat's.

'We have not been introduced,' said the Green Man defensively.

'Oh, yes we have,' said the Devil, 'We're re-introduced every day of our lives.'

'Your place is in hell,' said the Green Man. 'Each to his element.'

'My place is with you,' said the Devil, 'I'm in my element with you. Every minute of the day. You can't get away from me. Look at those mice and those mermaids.'

'I spared the mice and the mermaids,' said the Green Man.

'Only just,' said the Devil, 'and your daughters did the clearing up. And what about your twelve sons?'

The Green Man fell silent. 'They are grown and flown,' he said. 'We are part of one another, therefore I have no guilt. I cannot go searching for them specifically. It isn't my destiny.'

'I have things to show you,' said the Devil. 'Perhaps you will accompany me to the moon, and find your destiny?'

On the moon the two twins sat side by side upon a rock and looked down upon the beautiful blue planet, so small in the sky.

'Yours,' said the Devil.

'It's been said before,' said the Green Man. 'Are the conditions the same?'

'Yours,' said the Devil again. 'Here's a zapp. Zapp it.'

'No,' said the Green Man.

'Why not? The earth has never been good to you. Look how you've worked for it and loved it. Do you imagine that places love you back? A landscape doesn't hesitate to destroy you. Your fate has been predicted since humanity could predict. You are touched with death. You are strangled by the living green. Look at the old carvings of you in all those churches and ancient palaces. In the end you will vanish from the earth.'

'I keep away from carvings.'

'The Greeks and Romans made stone effigies of you and the Christians made copies. Over half the world there are images of you with vines growing like moustaches out of your nostrils. Then from your ears, and even your tongue. Sometimes they even grow from your eyeballs. Your beautiful face is the face of grief. You are born to die. It is eternal sorrow that stares through the leaves. Sad and bound is the Green Man.'

'There is Christ,' said the Green Man.

'Is there?' asked the Devil.

*

den 1998

'Go on, zapp them,' said the Devil, 'Zapp them all, down there. You could.'

'There are my sons and daughters.'

'They don't care for you. You are nothing but a nuisance to them. You embarrass your sons. Your death would be welcome. You are a burden and a reproach.'

'They are part of me, my twelve sons. And my four daughters.'

'I'm part of you, too,' said the Devil, 'let 'em go.'

The Green Man sat silent.

'The moon is clean and free,' said the Devil, 'untainted as yet by human wickedness. You, with your green fingers, could bring here the first new shoot which would break into grasses and flowers, crops and forests. You could create a new world, perfect in God's sight. You yourself could be God. The wilderness would flower like no earthly paradise. Let the old world go.'

'I'd need the earth for back-up,' said the Green Man weakening, and as he said it some moss that had become caught in his hair from a low branch of the apple tree slid out of his leafy curls. A spider that had been living in the moss began a hasty thread from the curls to the moon-dust.

The Green Man watched the spider which went tearing about here and there, bouncing up and down like a yo-yo. The Green Man held out his finger and tweaked the spider back, and for want of anywhere better, flicked him up into his hair again. 'I cannot leave the greenwood,' he said.

'Almost everything else has,' said the Devil, 'and what you mean "Greenwood"? D'you think you're Shakespeare or something?'

'I'm something,' said the Green Man.

'You're nothing at all,' said the Devil, 'You don't know who you are or what you are. All this about elements, you don't know your own. Nobody believes in you. You're kidsbook stuff. They don't even call pubs after you any more. They change them to something from Walt Disney. The only ones who go on about you now are Black-Magic freaks who think you're something to do with me.'

'Not quite the only ones,' said the Green Man.

'Well - who else? The has-beens, the hoi-polloi, the folk historians?'

'Sadie and Billy believed in me,' said the Green Man, 'and Patsie. And the corn-chandler.'

'Who-he?' asked the Devil, commonly.

'The water-voles, the geese, the mice and the mermaids believe in me.'

'Oh Christ!' said the Devil.

'Oh *what?*' said the Green Man.

The Devil stirred up the moon-dust with his finger, gently so that the pressure didn't bounce him away. He seemed unenthusiastic about answering.

'D'you really think Christ cares about you?' he said at last. 'Think what a world you live in. Think what a wonder it could be and what he's allowed you to do with it. I tell you - forget him. Zapp it. And him. Create the moon.'

'The moon is created.'

'Re-create it. Clothe it. Beautify it above the earth. Look at the potential, man. Look around you. A pure new architecture, rivers of silver, mountains of gold. After you've moved the space-trash of course.'

'I would spawn more.'

'Technology, man, technology. Enlightened clearances create a world of light. Get the straw from your hair. You spend whole days, whole years, scything the grass of an orchard nobody needs. You can get bags of apples half the price in the supermarket. And think of the space on the moon. You could do it. With my help. All you have to do is believe in me.'

The Green Man tried now, seriously, to consider the Devil's rational good sense and to analyze what the earth and the moon really meant for him. He thought of the moon's calm light as it sailed above the branches of the orchard.

'It's not for me to change it,' he said.

'I'm disappointed in you,' said the Devil.

'I'm disappointed in *you*,' said the Green Man.

'But *why?*' asked the Devil with his sweet and loving smile.

'You're nothing but my shabby self,' said the Green Man. 'You're the dark side of my soul. You're *déjà vu.*'

The Devil then threw a rock at him and vanished and the Green Man in an instant was back in the orchard under a Ribston Pippin. It was cold and raining and the fruits above his head looked ungrateful and sour. He found himself weeping and weak.

'I must sleep,' he said, 'Here in the grass and the rain. When I wake perhaps I won't feel that it's been a defeat,' and he fell asleep in the grass that would be cut for hay on Saturday.

The spider walked out of his hair and spun a beautiful web across his tired eyes.

Fedden 1998

5

The Green Man Attends a Place
of Worship

At harvest festival, like many farmers since its ancient institution and maybe only out of pagan habit, the Green Man sometimes goes to church. He goes to the early morning service where there are few people. The church has always been lovingly decorated for harvest with flowers and vines and bines and trails of hops. There is bread plaited or covered in cob-nuts or marked into gold squares. There are no sheaves of corn these days, but tins of baked beans that are later taken to patients in hospital. Patients in hospital would be bewildered by sheaves. They are rather bewildered by baked beans and usually hand them over to their visitors. The visitors take them home and give them to their children when there has to be a contribution to the next school fête. The baked beans bought at the fête will be half-price and often come back to church for the next harvest festival. This is country life.

The Green Man is hard to discern among the hop bines and the baked beans in the church at harvest, but he is there if you look hard enough. He doesn't sit in the body of the church but tends to be up in the chancel, leaning against a pillar, peering through the decorations of harvest green and gold. Up above him on a corbel (c. 1220) his own effigy looks down. It is his own head, wrapped in vine leaves like a Greek dinner.

The Green Man's head, so beautiful, passionate, tormented, ardent is being eaten up by oak leaves. He stares down at the living Green Man – who is listening gratefully to the Collect – and around the church which is his prison.

'I see myself everywhere,' says the living Green Man. 'First in the orchard,' he says, 'then on the moon. Good likenesses, though by no means exact. And I'm supposedly defunct. I am seldom noticed, and when I am noticed everyone sees someone different, a scarecrow, a saint, a devil or "That old guy on the farm; bit out of his element these days. Belongs to the past." They do not *peruse* my face. Sometimes they see me, sometimes they don't.'

'The fruits in their season,' intones the parson.

At the Gospel the Green Man turns to face the east end of the church as has been his medieval way. This brings him to face his companions along the pew. It is the choir-stall pew of Transept Manor. Lord Transept and Lady Serena Transept, their cheerful cousin and the dog, stand in a row. All remain face forward in the aristocratic low-church way, except the dog who decides to face west and wag its tail at the Green Man. The cheerful cousin waves her handkerchief at him.

After the service Lady Serena Transept, tall, flat and slender as her ancestor who lies on top of a nearby tomb in wimple, camisole and long stone robe (and who looks much like her except that Lady Serena has a long hooky nose and the ancestor's was snipped off into a Cromwellian pocket) Lady Serena Transept turns to the Green Man and lays a long-fingered paw upon his Sunday-best green tweed arm. 'Come to breakfast,' she says.

So they all set forth to Transept Manor, Lady Serena driving fast through the swishing puddles of the mile-long avenue of dead elms. Lord Transept broods alongside and the cousin sits in the back humming hymns with the dog, who looks delightedly at the Green Man who follows on his bicycle. In the manor kitchen they drink tea and eat toast and the cousin selects the numbers for her lottery ticket and the dog lies ecstatic in the Green Man's lap. His lordship hangs in looming thought and Lady Serena strokes the back of the Green Man's hand.

'I never thought to meet you,' she said, 'I've looked up at you for years on the corbel.'

'Corbels and capitals, tympana and misericords,' says the Green Man, 'I'm all over the place, yet nobody knows who I am. I am not all stone. I come to church for all the great festivals.'

Fedden 1998

'I know. I have seen you. So has my dog, but we never dared speak. I *feel* that I know you. I *know* that I know you. One knows a lot about the person one prays next to.'

'Marmalade,' says his lordship.

'Tootle-oo,' sings the cousin.

The dog sighs.

Outside the rain has stopped and the drops on the bumpy diamonds of the window panes turn the day to wet gold. Sunshine breaks across the cauliflower fields and lights a lantern-yard of fruit trees, ten miles of hop-gardens, three needle spires and a stretch of Roman road on the horizon where big lorries and tractor-vans roll along like toys.

The beams in the manor house kitchen are made from oaks that may have dropped acorns on legionaries. Whoever decided to make a kitchen of them didn't bother to take off all the bark. There are bumps and sawn circles where branches have been trimmed off to be slung onto fires that roasted oxen. The Green Man, surveying these timbers, reflects that there is nothing like them on the moon.

'Soon we shall *all* go to the moon,' says the jolly cousin.

His lordship says 'These days I am only able to put one foot in front of another.'

'Sometimes,' says his sister, 'I'm afraid you can't even do that.'

This scene in the manor kitchen the Green Man finds very comforting.

Lady Serena Transept walks with the Green Man part of the way home. He pushes his bicycle beside her along the avenue and she jumps the puddles like a giraffe (and she all of ninety) her spindle legs in thick, lace-patterned stockings.

'We are both old things,' she says. 'Antiques. I and his lordship and the Manor will soon be gone, and all our kind.'

'And no doubt, I,' says the Green Man.

'Oh, I don't think so,' she says. 'I'd doubt that very seriously.'

Fedden 1998

fedden 1998

6

THE GREEN MAN AND

THE LOSS-ADJUSTER'S WOMAN

The Green Man is in the coppice, lean as a sapling, pausing with his axe, peering from his deep-set eyes through the silver branches. Who is this walking over the meadow towards his house?

She disappears in a fold of the field where the house lies, and after some time she re-emerges and walks towards him. She has passed through his house, front door to back, for both always stand open. Here she comes on her high heels, a thin snake smoking a cigarette which she throws away into the coppice. The Green Man is invisible in the bouquets of the ash clumps, his face dappled by the flickering leaves that caress his cheeks, and sweep out from around his eyebrows. *'Who's this then?'*

He watches carefully to make sure that the cigarette lies dead in the wood chippings and the wood anemones. There is no glow.

She passes. She has a mean look. She wears town clothes, not warm enough, but very neat. She places her feet with care and they take her out of sight, down to the great May trees and beyond; beyond the struggling elms and the whispering poplars, out over the marsh. There she goes. Only a dot now. Over the marsh to the sea-side.

Fedden 1998

Now she is returning. She passes through the coppice again and he sees her little watchful face. It is a closed face. The face of a spy.

This time she side-steps his hidden house and soon he hears a motor starting up and driving away. The silence flows over the land again to be broken before long by the Green Man as he flings his axe against the sapling stalks in rhythmic chopping.

Working in the coppice, several days later he hears the sound of a more powerful motor stop outside his house and much later drive away. But there is often heavy agricultural traffic in the lanes. He works until nightfall, and the wind changes and comes off the sea. He feels cold. He walks home thinking, 'I shall sleep indoors tonight.' He has his axe over his shoulder and he whistles for his dog but the dog doesn't come. He thinks of hot porridge and hot tea and maybe hot whisky before bed.

But there is no bed. There is no couch. There is no table. There is no chair. Gone is the small wooden-handled herb-chopper of ancient design, the barometer given him by the peripatetic academic folklorist, the hat that once belonged to Oliver Cromwell, willed to him by an earlier Lord Transept. Gone are the books from the shelf, the brown lustre jug from the dresser, the comb stuck with sea-shells he bought at the door but has never liked. Gone is the black iron kettle on the chain and the iron griddle that hung from the rafters, the great black court-cupboard mysteriously carved in Bremen, and the jerry-pot of Meissen. Gone is the dog.

The Green Man walks in the wind calling for the dog. When at last he returns, he makes porridge but not in the sooty pot with the heavy silver lining, for that is gone.

There remains one very old hearth-mat made from coloured scraps of cloth from God knows how many countries, and the Green Man wraps this about him and sleeps upon the floor.

In the morning, or perhaps several mornings later, come some daughters, lovely as lilies. They see upon the floor this long roly-poly with head and feet stuck out at either end and all the shreddy garment-patches in between. There is a scrap of eighteenth-century smock, a nineteenth century bloomer, a snicket of liberty-bodice still with one small pearl button. There is the edge of a milkmaid's petticoat and a glimpse of lavender silk from the bride's dress of who knows who in the Green Man's history and all the women in it. His green feet are sockless for his socks are gone. His green hair floats about, for gone is his limpet-covered comb. The Green Man in his bedding-roll is like a multi-coloured almond-slice in the window of an eccentric pastry-cook.

The dog, all burrs and sorrow, lies close beside him on the floor.

Mugged! Dead! Police! Robbers!

Certainly robbers.

Retribution! Revenge!

But the Green Man sits up on an apple-box and takes a mug of tea and picks burrs off the dog. The dog can't stop shivering.

'Oh, we'll catch them,' says the policeman, a fishy, flashy fellow who has a past, and doubtful friends. The Green Man has often heard him sniffing about. 'And we'll soon get the Loss-Adjuster in.'

The Green Man is unaware of loss-adjusters and presumes them to be philosophers.

'You might also like to see a counsellor,' says the young police-girl, overweight and gorgeous. '*I could counsel you,*' her eyes say to the exotic feral eyes of the Green Man. 'Give me your knowledge,' say her eyes to the eyes of the Green Man. '*After hours.*'

'But I have suffered no loss,' says the Green Man. 'I shall miss the little herb-chopper and my socks, for they were knitted by someone close to me. But that is all.'

'He enjoys frugality,' say the daughters putting up a new bed and couch, setting stainless steel on the shelf. 'He is in his element when he's away from plenty.'

The Green Man strokes his dog and wishes they would all go away.

'Do you bring a charge then?' asked the policeman.

'Yes,' say the daughters.

'No,' says the Green Man. 'No charge. Free for all.'

Then, looking at the policeman, he says, 'I shall lose nothing.'

'I'd not count on that, grandad. There was the big antiques fair at Newark this week and all will be gone to Holland in containers now. You'll be insured of course? The Loss-Adjuster will see to you!'

The Green Man is not conversant with matters of insurance. Each to his element.

The police-girl cannot keep away. She calls early and late, but after a time she does not find the Green Man at home. She calls to him across the marshes, but there is no reply. He sleeps out in the coppices among the wood anemones, and relies on Indian take-aways from next-door farmers, old and young Mr Jackson. 'Hello?' she calls. 'Are you there? It's me. Pearly.' She wanders dreaming through the coppice in her black, police-girl shoes. She thinks about him all the time. She is never to meet such another. Over the dykes, down to the sea she goes, and the sharp grasses prick against her strapping legs. One day she leaves a daring note on the new plastic table in the Green Man's kitchen, with a box of chocolates and a dozen pairs of socks marked 'nylon-rich'.

The Green Man doesn't understand the note, feeds the chocolates to the dog. The socks revolt him.

One day, comes the first woman again on her high heels, over the meadow. She looks left and right, left and right, and smokes her cigarette. When she reaches the coppice she stands for a while to grow accustomed to its green light and sees the Green Man standing there. She makes to throw down the cigarette but then decides to rub it out on the sole of her shoe. She puts it in her pocket. 'Hi,' she says. She seems uneasy. He does not speak.

'My partner is the Loss-Adjuster and he's down in the car waiting.'

'I have not suffered loss.'

'You've been victimised. You've been done over. And it's someone who knows everything about you.'

'*Everything* about me?'

She blushes and pretends to be bored. 'He's come to make an assessment.'

'An assessment of me?'

'He is the policeman's twin brother.'

'Ah!'

There falls a silence, until the Green Man walks across to her through the wood-shavings that scent the air among the flowers. There are bluebells now. Such bluebells! Smoke on summer eves. The scent of bluebells, the Green Man tells her, lasts for one week only.

The Green Man carries his glistening axe over his shoulder and comes close to the woman and looks down on her. He examines her troubled eyes. Then he takes the axe from his shoulder and in both hands holds it high above his head.

She cannot move.

Then he places the axe in her stained hands, with their chipped red nails and says 'Take this, too.'

She throws it to the ground and runs away, stumbling back across the meadow.

As she passes the house the dog shoots out and goes for her heels, snap snap. He remembers her. He remembers, too, the Loss-Adjuster who is sitting in the car.

The Loss-Adjuster is not keen to get out.

'He won't take money,' says the Loss-Adjuster's woman, falling into the seat beside him, the dog raising merry hell.

'Why you all over 'im? Let 'im be,' says the Loss-Adjuster. He smells of guilt and sweating fear that glistens on his cheeks.

'He could get us caught,' squeaks his woman.

'Get on. 'e's lunatic.'

'I don't know what he is.' She is crying.

The Green Man stands now on the rise behind his invisible house, and watches them. The evening sun flames on his woodland limbs. His axe gleams. His hair blows green in the wind.

''e's from back in the Sixties. 'e's an old drug-addict. 'e's damaged,' says the Loss-Adjuster. 'There's stories about 'im. Forget it can't you?'

'We've got to get it all back to him. He's bad news.'

''e doesn't want it . Pearl told us. She's been leaving him notes. She's gone soft on him.'

Then the Loss-Adjuster's woman is filled with raving jealousy and tries to get out of the car. 'I must go to the Green Man,' she screams and the sweaty Loss-Adjuster socks her and starts the car and tries to drive it away down the lanes where sometimes farm-machinery passes along, each machine the length and height and weight of a street of houses. One of these in a moment meets the Loss-Adjuster and his Moll on the corner of a field of flax. The flax is oh, such a colour! It is a more shadowy and gentler blue even than bluebells, blue as a tender evening sky and now splattered all over with scarlet.

The police-girl Pearl is quickly on the scene. She begs again to be allowed to counsel the Green Man, this time in his double tragedy; but he looks over her head, far far away.

'Don't you care about *anything*,' she weeps. 'Why can't you need comfort?'

So he takes her home for a while, then makes her some tea in a tin mug and sends her away with the multi-coloured rug, his last treasure. The rug is made of patches of paduasoy and glazed linen and sprig-muslin snips; of velveteen and taffeta and tussore, of here and there a wiry shred of a hair-shirt; but much point d'esprit and threadwork and blackwork and bead work and hedebo; and rich lazy-daisy and faggoting and Venetian toile cirée. The old rug is strongly backed with flour bags, and she keeps it all her life.

7

The Green Man Meets his Maker

The gold and rose coloured autumn is gone and in November come the wind and the rain and the Green Man's twelve sons in a minibus. He sees it from his kitchen window, and closes his eyes. In they all stream. 'What a disgrace! You look ill! You look haggard! Who looks after you? Where are our sisters?'

'They are on a short holiday in the south of France.'

'Lucky for some. *They* don't work like we do. *We* can't afford holidays in the south of France. And how stupid, too, "south of France", at this time of the year! You are living so poor. You need paint and wallpaper. Your roof is full of holes. You will shame us in the neighbourhood. What's for dinner?'

'I'm afraid I no longer eat dinner. I no longer need it.'

'You are undernourished. You have leaves in your hair. Let me get on the blower for supplies, carpenters, painters. Amenities.'

'Amenities?'

'The electricity board, the telephone centre, the television and video shop.'

'And to the Authorities,' says the eldest son. 'There are excellent homes for the elderly.'

'I am not elderly,' said the Green Man, 'I am the Green Man.'

'Hello? Hello? Yes, he needs help. He is alone. Practically *unfurnished*. His hair needs cutting. We think his mind is affected.'

'Out!' shouts the Green Man. 'The lot of you. Back to your element,' and he picks up a flail that leans by the back door and begins to strike out about him, clubbing some of them on the head.

They all scatter in their sharp suits, clutching their mobile phones. All except the youngest who turns back to say, 'Sorry it's been so long, Dad. It's so easy to forget the passage of time.'

'I've stood so long in the passage of time,' says the Green Man, 'It is my home sweet home.'

'Can you manage?' asks the youngest son; and another one round about number six, who's not altogether bad, peeps round the door and fingers his club tie. 'Have you enough money?'

'Money has never been a trouble to me.'

'Have you enough food?' and he lifts the lid of the flour crock and sees the drum marked MOUSE POISON.

'Mouse poison in the flour crock!' cries the eldest, awful son with his blow-dried hair, coming back into the kitchen, 'That does it. Not fit to live alone' and he picks up the drum and makes off with it to the minibus where the rest of the brothers are glaring through the windows, terrified.

'We'll take it back to the corn-chandler and get him to send you some bread,' says the kindly, though feeble, youngest son.

'He doesn't deliver.'

'Oh, I'm sure that he would.'

'Goodbye,' says the Green Man, stern as Ulysses.

He watches the minibus depart, driven very erratically and bad-temperedly by the eldest son. The youngest son waves from the window.

'Thank God,' says the Green Man and lies down on his new couch and listens to the silence. After a time, into the silence, a wind begins to blow. It crosses his fields, a peculiarly soft wind for winter. The Green Man sleeps.

Then the Green Man has a dream. He dreams that the wind has strengthened and is tearing at his house in the fold of the fields, and that he hears branches and sheds come crashing down. He dreams that he goes to fasten the clattery window in the kitchen, and there outside, beneath a leafless tree in the apple orchard, stands a figure who looks as if he owns the place. Before shutting the window the Green Man shouts, 'Get off my land.'

Then he wraps himself in an extra sack and goes outdoors.

'What do you think you're doing in my orchard?' he cries.

'I'm standing on next year's daffodils,' says the man.

The man's clothes do not blow in the mighty wind. Otherwise his figure is much like that of the Green Man. He is tall and lean and wears something like the sack. This time it is certainly not the Devil.

The Green Man thinks once more, '*Now I must be seeing through a looking-glass*,' and he walks right round the man. The man's hair is longer than the Devil's so that the Green Man cannot examine the lines in his neck, but nevertheless he thinks, 'This is myself.' When he comes round front again however and looks into the man's eyes, he sees that the man is Christ.

The Green Man falls to his knees, but Christ raises him up.

'Your troubles are over,' says Christ.

'You mean I am about to die?'

'I mean that there is no death,' says Christ, 'Today you will be with me in paradise.'

'But, I'm the Green Man. The earth is my element. This is my tragedy. You know this. I am not yours. I am bound and tied. I am from some other old place. The very meaning of me is not known. You do not include me.'

Christ said, 'The Green Man is no enemy of Christ.'

The Green Man woke from his dreams and the wind was not the soft wind to which he had fallen asleep. It was shrieking and howling as it had done in the dream orchard.

It was daylight. The Green Man went to fasten the clattering window where nobody was standing under the trees.

'I shall eat some bread,' said the Green Man. He felt very tired. 'And I shall drink some water.' Then he remembered that the flour crock was empty and the water down in the field dyke felt far away.

So he thought, '*I'll rest a bit longer*,' and lay down again on the couch. Soon he began to feel peaceful. 'I shall wait here for Death,' he said, 'Here it comes.'

Soon, far away down the lanes, he heard the sound of Death approaching. It was a great, black Yamaha. Its rider sat astride it, a black figure in black vizor and black armour. Black gauntlets grasped black handlebars. The noise of the great bike seemed to silence the wind.

'It is here,' said the Green Man as the motorbike shuddered, surged and stopped at his gate. He walked to his front door and opened it on the black day.

Death pushed his steed right to the Green Man's threshold. Fastened to its flank was a box with lid and a strap.

'*Too small for a coffin,*' thought the Green Man, '*Maybe it's for my ashes.*'

'Can I bring it round the back?' asked Death, 'Just in case it gets nicked-at-all?'

'*Nicked?*' said the Green Man, 'I don't think Nick's here any more. He's gone. You needn't fear him. This is a good place now, and I am ready to die.'

'To *die?*' said Death, 'Oh come on now.' And Death removed the black helmet and unzipped the black leathers.

Out stepped a girl like a spring flower, and all of sixteen. 'I am the corn-chandler's daughter,' she said, 'and I've brought you some bread.'

They looked, and they loved.

'It is a miracle,' said the corn-chandler's daughter in the Green Man's arms.

'It is heaven!' she said on the Green Man's couch.

'And it is impossible,' she said in the Green Man's bed, 'for I am to be married on Saturday to Jackson your next-door farmer.'

And she was. The bells of the steeple rang out for her (a quiet bride) on the Saturday afternoon.

Earlier that week, one bright and frosty day, they had begun to toll for many hours, a peal for each year of the Green Man's life. The mice heard it in the pockets of the old macintosh on the back of his kitchen door. The water-voles and the swans heard it in the dykes. The geese heard it, flying south. The sea-gulls heard it. (They think they are nobody's fool, and guessed what it was) Sadie and Billy and Patsie and their grandchildren heard it on the farms around and said, 'How endlessly it tolls. It must be for the Green Man.'

Deep in the winter sea the mermaids heard it, and didn't much care.

The twelve sons didn't hear it because they were all at foreign conferences, but the four daughters on a cold beach in France heard it in their hearts. A shiver passed among them and they looked at one another sadly. Lady Serena Transept and her cousin and the dog heard it and went specially to sit in the Manor pew to listen. Occasionally, as they sat there, the dog howled. Above them, the head on the corbel peered through its leaves to watch the ringers and Lord Transept, who

Fedden 1998

had asked particularly to toll the final knell.

In the high street of the market town the corn chandler heard it, and he smiled. He knew the future, being a reading man.

And was unsurprised, therefore, some years later, a green-eyed grandson on his knee, to hear that somebody going through the lanes towards the tip to dump his Christmas tree, had seen a shadow standing in the fields.